TRAILBLAZERS
of the MODERN WORLD

OPRAH WINFREY

By Jean F. Blashfield

WORLD ALMANAC® LIBRARY

Please visit our web site at: www.worldalmanaclibrary.com
For a free color catalog describing World Almanac® Library's list
of high-quality books and multimedia programs, call 1-800-848-2928 (USA)
or 1-800-387-3178 (Canada). World Almanac® Library's fax: (414) 332-3567.

Library of Congress Cataloging-in-Publication Data available upon request from publisher.
Fax (414) 336-0157 for the attention of the Publishing Records Department.

ISBN 0-8368-5087-4 (lib. bdg.)
ISBN 0-8368-5247-8 (softcover)

First published in 2003 by
World Almanac® Library
330 West Olive Street, Suite 100
Milwaukee, WI 53212 USA

Copyright © 2003 by World Almanac® Library.

Project manager: Jonny Brown
Project editor: Betsy Rasmussen
Design and page production: Scott M. Krall
Photo research: Diane Laska-Swanke
Indexer: Carol Roberts

Photo credits: © Evan Agostini/Getty Images: 40 top; © AP/Wide World Photos: 6, 8, 21, 23, 26, 27 both, 30, 33, 34, 43
bottom; © Bettmann/CORBIS: 5, 12 top, 13; © Tim Boyle/Getty Images: 43 top; © Manny Ceneta/Getty Images: 40
bottom; © Jeff Christensen/Reuters/Getty Images: 31; © Diane L. Cohen/Getty Images: 41; Courtesy of Getty Images:
38 top; © Gini Holland: 11, 12 bottom, 28; © Hulton Archive/Getty Images: 17, 18; © Cynthia Johnson/Getty Images: 32;
© David Keeler/Getty Images: 29; © Barry King/Getty Images: 42; © Diane Laska-Swanke: 14; Photofest: 4, 24 both, 36,
37 bottom; © Robin Platzer/Getty Images: 39; © Reuters/Jim Bourg/Getty Images: 25; © Reuters/Getty Images: 35;
© Reuters/Rose Prouser/Getty Images: cover; © Mike Segar/Reuters/Getty Images: 38 bottom; © Touchstone
Pictures/Courtesy of Getty Images: 37 top

Printed in the United States of America

1 2 3 4 5 6 7 8 9 07 06 05 04 03

TABLE of CONTENTS

Words that appear in the glossary are printed in **boldface** type the first time they occur in the text.

CHAPTER 1

EVERYBODY HAS A STORY

Oprah Winfrey was one of the most powerful women in the world as the twenty-first century started.

She got her start by acting out little plays for the animals on her grandparents' farm in Mississippi. Today, twenty-six million people in the United States and millions more in 119 countries around the world watch her television program, *The Oprah Winfrey Show*. Over two million people subscribe to her magazine, *O*, and millions have watched her movies. Her **charitable** gifts have been received by grateful people in this country and abroad. It has been said that if she ran for president, she would be elected, no doubt about it.

Oprah Winfrey, who is perhaps the best known African American after Dr. Martin Luther King Jr., is an amazing trailblazer. In late 2002, *Fortune* magazine placed a value of almost one billion dollars on Oprah's enterprises. *Life* magazine called her "America's Most Powerful Woman," and *Newsweek* called her the "Woman of the Century."

First Name Only

Oprah Winfrey is one of the few people in the world whom everybody recognizes by her first name alone. There is no doubt who you mean when you say "Oprah." Because of this name recognition, books about her usually refer to her by only her first name. In this book, as in life, she's known simply as Oprah.

Others simply call Oprah a "talk-show host." Talk shows are radio or television programs on which the host holds conversations with various people, often celebrities. Until the *Oprah Winfrey Show* began, Phil Donahue was the "king" of the talk shows. He walked among the audience holding a microphone so that people could comment or ask questions of the show's guests.

Oprah, too, encourages her audience to take part in the discussions she has with her guests. These guests are often famous. George W. Bush was on her show just before he was elected president. Poet and writer Maya Angelou has been on the show many times, and she and Oprah have become friends. Actors, singers, writers, politicians, and newsmakers of all kinds have been on Oprah's stage. But just as often, her guests are average people with average problems. She laughs, jokes, and cries with them. She also asks the questions that people watching from home would ask if they could. Oprah is skilled at getting people to tell their stories. In fact, she is so good at it that her name was turned into a verb. In the 1990s, first teenagers and then adults began to use the phrase "to oprah," meaning to question a person closely until all the intimate details are revealed.

How does she do it? She listens. She doesn't think about anything else when she's talking to her guests. She told *Harper's Bazaar* magazine: "The best way to connect with people is to understand that everybody has a story. A story that is as painful, joyful, confused, and as hopeful as your own. Know that and listen."

But Oprah is so much more than a talk-show host. She uses her popular television program to encourage her audience to take personal and

Phil Donahue, seen here in 1977, was the "king" of talk shows before Oprah got her start.

social action. She encourages individuals to lead healthy lifestyles, both physically and emotionally. She asks them to make the world a better place by giving time and money to those less fortunate.

So what is Oprah's story? It is one of determination. The Mississippi house where Oprah spent her first six years is gone now, but the country road on which it stood has been renamed Oprah Winfrey Road as recognition of the determination that allowed her to escape a difficult childhood and develop into the successful businesswoman and **humanitarian** that she is today.

Texas governor George W. Bush appeared on *The Oprah Winfrey Show* just before he was elected president of the United States.

Oprah Gail Winfrey was born on January 29, 1954, near Kosciusko, in central Mississippi. Her great-aunt chose the name Orpah for her, after a character in the biblical book of Ruth. When the name was put on a birth certificate, however, it was misspelled, making it Oprah. By the time Oprah's mother, nineteen-year-old Vernita Lee, gave birth to her, Oprah's father, Vernon Winfrey, was in the armed forces, stationed far away. He did not even know that he had a daughter until he received a letter from Vernita asking him to send clothes. Oprah's parents never married.

Vernita and Oprah lived with Vernita's parents, Hattie Mae and Earless (pronounced "UR-luhss"). Her grandparents' land was little more than two acres (.8 hectare), but it supported their small farm. Oprah had no playmates there, so instead, she put on plays and shows for the pigs and chickens that she helped care for.

While Oprah enjoyed her farmyard productions, she enjoyed books even more. By the time Oprah was three years old, her grandmother had taught her to read—even the complex words and phrases of the Bible. Oprah liked to memorize and recite Bible passages. Her first public speech was at age three, when she charmed the congregation in church with a dramatic, clearly spoken retelling of the Easter story.

Oprah's grandmother—whom Oprah called "momma"—took care of Oprah, but she did not give the little girl any hugs or kisses. When Hattie Mae did touch Oprah, it was usually to whip her. Today, we know these beatings were child **abuse**. In later years, Oprah would angrily disagree with people who said that physically

Racism in Kosciusko

Oprah didn't have much experience with racism, growing up in the Kosciusko region of Mississippi. Another famous native of Kosciusko did, however. James Meredith gained national attention in 1962 as the first African American admitted to the University of Mississippi. His appearance on campus led to riots that left two people dead and many injured. Military troops had to be called in to stop the violence.

James Meredith, a native of Kosciusko, Mississippi, was the first African American to graduate from the University of Mississippi, in 1963. When he entered the previously all-white college, violent riots erupted.

punishing children was a way to show them that you love them. Hattie Mae and Earless were not loving grandparents. But Oprah later recalled, "I am what I am because of my grandmother. My strength. My sense of reasoning. Everything. All that was set by the time I was six."

There may not have been much love, but there was plenty to eat. Oprah grew up expecting large, varied meals on the table. Food became very important to the girl. She used food as a substitute for love.

Learning was also important to Oprah. When Oprah started kindergarten, she quickly became bored with the lessons the nonreading kids did in class. She wrote to the teacher: "Dear Miss New: I do not think I belong here." Clearly, any kindergartner who could already write such a message indeed did not belong there. Oprah was transferred immediately into the first grade.

THE MOVE TO MILWAUKEE

Oprah was six when her mother decided to get married. Vernita had her parents send Oprah to Milwaukee to live with her. The marriage didn't happen, however, and, for the next eight years, Oprah lived in a single-parent home in poverty.

Moving from her grandparents' isolated farm in Mississippi to her mother's home in Wisconsin was a big change for Oprah. She went from a rural environment with strong discipline to a small apartment where she was usually ignored. She came from a community where race made no difference, to one where most African Americans lived in a **ghetto**.

Heading North

When Oprah was four, her mother left her with her grandparents and moved north. Between 1900 and 1960, almost five million African Americans moved north from the southern United States in what has been called the Great Migration. Vernita Lee was part of that migration, hoping to find a better life in a northern city. Hundreds of thousands of African Americans made new homes in Chicago, but Vernita Lee went farther north to Milwaukee, Wisconsin.

Vernita Lee had little time or attention for Oprah. She worked hard as a housemaid, and she liked to go out at night. Soon after Oprah moved to Milwaukee, her mother gave birth to another daughter, Patricia. With seven years between them, Oprah and Patricia had little in common. Oprah's half-sister had lighter skin and was quite beautiful. Young Oprah was called "the smart one," and she was sure that wasn't as good as being "the pretty one." Later, Vernita had another child, a boy named Jeffrey.

Before starting third grade (she skipped second grade), Oprah was sent to Nashville, Tennessee, to live with her father. Vernon Winfrey left the army in 1955 and moved to Nashville. There, he opened a barber shop and a small grocery store. He also was elected to the town council. He married a woman named Zelma, who became Oprah's stepmother.

Talking for a Living

Oprah made regular visits to her father in Nashville. During one visit, when she was twelve, a church paid her a great deal of money to speak to the congregation. She enjoyed it. That night, she told her father that that was what she wanted to do for a living—to be paid to talk.

Unlike her mother, Vernon and Zelma Winfrey paid a great deal of attention to Oprah. They put strict limits on where she could go and what she could do. They also paid attention to her schoolwork. Zelma found that Oprah hadn't yet learned the multiplication tables, which third graders in Nashville had already learned. Zelma spent the summer teaching her to multiply.

After a year in Nashville, Oprah went back to Milwaukee for the summer. Because her mother still had hopes of all her children living together with her, she persuaded Oprah to stay when school began in the fall.

In her mother's tiny apartment, many men came and went. One evening, when she was nine, Oprah was being "taken care of" by a nineteen-year-old cousin. He **raped** the bewildered and horrified girl. Oprah knew that what had happened was wrong. She was afraid that she was responsible somehow for letting it happen. She decided that no one must ever know. When other male visitors and relatives also abused her sexually, she became certain that she must be a bad person. She knew there were adults who were aware of what was happening, but they did nothing about it.

During the following years, she found that she could get attention from men by letting them sexually abuse her. No one told her that she had the right to say no. Oprah became quiet and withdrawn. She hid where she felt safe, in the world of books.

At Milwaukee's Lincoln High School, Oprah had a teacher named Gene Adams who recognized Oprah's intelligence. He arranged for her to attend Nicolet High School in the mostly white and comfortable suburb of Glendale. She had to take three buses to reach the school, and for the first time, she realized that she was poor. But the new experience was worth it, because she

Oprah attended Lincoln School in Milwaukee before a sympathetic teacher arranged for her to go to an integrated suburban school.

As a result of civil rights demonstrations, such as this one in New York, integration of black people into the use of public facilities became the law in the 1960s.

also learned that the ghetto in which she lived was not the whole world—there was a wider, much nicer world beyond it.

The year 1968 was the height of **integration** in schools around the nation. White students wanted to show their support by befriending African-American students, so Oprah was very popular. But her popularity contributed to her making some poor choices. Wanting to join the other students for pizza after school, Oprah began to steal from her mother. Then, following a fight with her mother, she ran away. After being away from home for several days, Oprah became terrified of returning. She finally went to her minister and asked him to contact her mother to see if she could come home.

When Oprah reached home, Vernita found out that the girl had a secret—she was pregnant. Vernita considered sending Oprah to a juvenile home but asked Vernon Winfrey to take her instead. Soon after arriving in Nashville, she gave birth to the baby, but it was **premature** and didn't survive.

Thirteen-year-old Oprah in her yearbook picture from Lincoln School in Milwaukee

A Celebrity Moment

Oprah says that when she ran away from home, she walked through downtown Milwaukee and came across singer Aretha Franklin getting out of a limousine. The thirteen-year-old ran up to Franklin and blurted out that she had been abandoned. The singer gave her a $100 bill, which Oprah used to live at a hotel for a couple of days, before deciding to return home.

Singer Aretha Franklin helped Oprah when the girl ran away from home.

After that, Vernon and Zelma made sure that Oprah's life changed. They insisted on knowing where she was and who she was with. They demanded that she go to church, be home at a certain time, and do her homework. With their guidance, Oprah became a different person.

The Truth Comes Out

The first full-scale biography of Oprah, written by Robert Waldon and published in 1987, made no mention of her teenage pregnancy. The pregnancy was revealed later by Oprah's half-sister, Patricia Lee, who sold the story to a **tabloid**. Though furious at the time, Oprah later said she was glad the story had come out. She always encourages people to tell the truth and felt bad about keeping such an important secret herself.

CHAPTER 3

WAKE UP, GIRL!

At the beginning, Oprah didn't like her father's strict rules, but she later saw him as the person who helped her to become a responsible human being. "He knew what he wanted and expected," she said, "and he would take nothing less."

Oprah was amazed when her father told her that Cs on her report card were not good enough—no one had ever cared before. Oprah took a good look at her life and decided that she would be the best that she could be. She started by studying harder and soon she began to get As. Oprah's stepmother asked Oprah to read books and write reports in addition to those Oprah completed for school. Zelma also encouraged Oprah to learn additional vocabulary words.

Oprah attended Nicolet High School in suburban Milwaukee long enough to discover that there was a world beyond the urban ghetto where she lived.

Taking guidance from Zelma Winfrey, Oprah (who called herself Gail at this time) also learned to dress differently. No longer did she wear the revealing clothes that she had chosen for herself in Milwaukee, and she stopped wearing so much makeup.

East High School in Nashville had only recently been integrated. Black and white teenagers were still learning to get along together. Many students were actively fighting for integration. There were also typical problems; some students used drugs. But Gail concentrated on her studies and stayed out of trouble. She also helped her father at his store and appeared in plays.

BECOMING A PUBLIC FIGURE

Oprah was active in Faith United Church, where she joined the youth group and often spoke in church. She was asked to speak at other churches, too, where she would often recite the series of seven sermons that black poet James Weldon Johnson wrote in the 1920s. Called "God's Trombones: Seven Negro Sermons in Verse," these dramatic readings brought audiences to the churches of Nashville to hear the talented teenager.

Oprah's talent resulted in her receiving traveling opportunities. At sixteen, she was invited to speak at a church in Los Angeles, California. While there, she was able to take a tour of Hollywood, and she returned home determined to become an actress. The next year, she was invited to join President Nixon's White House Conference of Youth, held in Estes Park, Colorado. She also represented Tennessee in the national **forensics** competition held at Stanford University in Palo Alto, California.

As a senior in high school, Oprah ran for student council president. Her opponents brought the subject of race into their campaign. Gail Winfrey, on the other hand, campaigned on issues important to all students and never mentioned race. She won the election.

Oprah's first exposure to broadcasting happened by accident when she was seventeen. In 1971, she was the only African American to enter the local Miss Fire Prevention contest. The judges of this beauty competition asked her what she would do if she were suddenly given a million dollars. In a flash, she ignored what she had previously planned to say and replied with total frankness: "I'd be a spending fool!" She won.

As Miss Fire Prevention, she was given a tour of WVOL, the black radio station that had sponsored her. In a light-hearted mood, the station manager asked the girl to read material into a microphone. Oprah had no time to get nervous. She did so well that the station offered her a job, reading news on the air. With this job as a newscaster, Oprah was able to stop working in her father's grocery store—a job she hated. She read the news after school every half hour until eight in the evening.

When it came time for Oprah to go to college, her father said that she could not go away. It had been only four years since her wild, unpredictable, and dangerous life in Milwaukee. He wanted to keep a close eye on her. Winning another beauty competition given by the Elks Club provided her with a four-year scholarship to the all-black Tennessee State University, right there in Nashville.

As a freshman in college, she entered the Miss Black Tennessee contest. In those days, African-American women were not allowed to take part in the Miss America Pageant, so black women had their own competition. She didn't expect to win, mainly because most of the other contestants were lighter skinned than she was, and she considered that an advantage. (Dark-skinned Oprah called herself a "fudge brownie" and the

Sojourner Truth—Oprah's Hero

When appearing in public, Oprah would often recite material about black women who were her heroes. Here is the story of one such hero.

Sojourner Truth (1797?–1883) was born a slave named Isabella Van Wagener, in New York state before slavery was outlawed there in 1828. In 1843, a voice told her to take the name Sojourner Truth and preach to the people. She wandered far and wide and gradually became a leader in the abolition movement to outlaw slavery. She worked with black abolitionist Frederick Douglass and white writer Harriet Beecher Stowe. At the Women's Rights Convention in 1851, she made a speech that Oprah would recite. A reporter recorded that Truth said: "That man over there says that women need to be helped into carriages, and lifted over ditches, and to have the best place everywhere. Nobody helps me any best place. And ain't I a woman?" The tall, striking woman raised her powerful arm. "Look at me! Look at my arm. I have plowed, I have planted and I have gathered into barns. And no man could head me. And ain't I a woman? . . . I have borne thirteen children, and seen most all sold off to slavery, and when I cried out with my mother's grief, none but Jesus heard me! And ain't I a woman?"

Sojourner Truth posed for this photograph about 1860.

Harriet Tubman had seen black slaves freed by the time this photo was taken about 1870.

Harriet Tubman—Oprah's Hero

Here is a story of another of Oprah's heroes.

Harriet Tubman (1820?–1913) was born a slave, in Maryland. In 1849, she succeeded in escaping the plantation where she lived. During the years before the Civil War, she secretly returned to Maryland nineteen times and led to freedom up to two hundred other slaves. Whispered word of her successes helped to expand the Underground Railroad, the routes along which slaves escaped to reach freedom in the North. During the Civil War, this brave woman served as a spy and scout in South Carolina. In 1869, the author of a book about Harriet Tubman gave her the name "Moses of Her People."

other girls "vanilla creams" and "gingerbreads.") But her lively personality and great talent gave her the prize.

While in college, Oprah became totally enamored of a young man named William Taylor. She wanted to marry him, but he refused to do so. Years later, Oprah was relieved that he had. If she had married then, her whole life would have been different.

As she had in grade school, Oprah spent most of her time in college alone, reading. She also was in many plays, because her major was speech and drama. She hoped to become an actress.

INTO TELEVISION

The local CBS television station in Nashville, WTVF-TV, called Oprah to see if she would audition for a job on the air. The people at the TV station, like the people at the radio station when she was in high school, knew that her voice and personality were ideal for broadcasting.

Becoming the first woman and the first black newscaster in Nashville, Oprah knew that she got the job just because it was considered correct to have an African American on the air. Such a person is often called a "**token** black." Oprah said, "I was a classic token, but I was one happy token."

She held the job for three years while she finished college. Then Oprah knew that she wanted to get out into the wider world—and away from her still-strict father. She began to send tapes of her television appearances to stations around the country. Baltimore, Maryland called. She was on her way.

CHAPTER 4

TALK IS "LIKE BREATHING"

Ready for adventure and a chance to live away from her family for the first time, twenty-two-year-old Oprah Winfrey headed for Baltimore, Maryland, and WJZ-TV. The TV station advertised her coming to Baltimore with a campaign that asked "What's an Oprah?" They hoped that viewers would be intrigued and tune in. Oprah didn't like the campaign. She would have preferred to enter Baltimore quietly.

Her job in Baltimore was similar to the one she had in Nashville, but Oprah had new problems. First, she had to work with another **anchor** person with whom she had no chemistry. They just couldn't relate to each other, and it showed. Second, she had no real professional training. And third, she tended to react to the news she was reading. She laughed at funny stories, sighed at touching ones, and cried at sad ones. She wanted to share feelings about the stories with her audience.

Powerful Perspective

During her years in Baltimore, Oprah fell in love with a man she has never named. Whenever he tried to break up with her, she saw herself as worthless, despite all her accomplishments. She told herself that if she didn't have a man in her life, she was nothing. So Oprah begged this man to stay with her.

Emerging from a period of depression after he walked away from her for good, Oprah realized that she "had given this man the power over my life. And I will never, never—as long as I'm black!—I will never give up my power to another person. Now I'm free. I'm soaring!"

The managers of WJZ-TV kept trying to remake Oprah into something that fit their image of what an anchorwoman should be. The news director even sent her to New York to get a permanent. The hairdresser left the chemicals on too long, even though Oprah kept telling her that they were burning her head. Several days later, her hair fell completely out. Oprah's head is large, and a wig to fit her could not be found. She had to wear scarves until her hair grew back. Years later, she told a reporter for *Ms.* magazine, "You learn a lot about yourself when you're bald and black and an anchorwoman in Baltimore.

In 1978, WJZ-TV management moved Oprah to a position as cohost on a talk show called *People Are Talking.* Oprah could finally be herself and say her own words instead of ones written for her. "This is what I really should have been doing all along," she said. "It was like breathing after suffocating for a long time!"

In 1985, Oprah was enjoying the success she had found in Chicago after some bitter experiences in Baltimore, Maryland.

There was chemistry between her and her cohost, Richard Sher. They encouraged each other to be the best they could be. They were funny together, and people enjoyed talking with them, just as they enjoyed talking with everyone who came into the studio.

News of the exciting change in *People Are Talking* spread. Soon everyone wanted to know who Oprah was interviewing that morning. Oprah discovered that the most interesting shows were with people who were slightly **controversial**.

Oprah and *People Are Talking* began to draw a bigger Baltimore audience than *The Phil Donahue Show*, which was on the air at the same time. She was having fun and earning plenty of money.

ON TO CHICAGO

In 1983, a member of Oprah's **production** staff in Baltimore, Debra DiMaio, got a job at WLS-TV in Chicago, producing a talk show called *A.M. Chicago*. It broadcast at 9 AM, right after *Good Morning America*, but it had never drawn a good audience.

Within days of DiMaio starting her new job, a cohost of *A.M. Chicago* moved to New York. DiMaio and Dennis Swanson, the station's general manager, decided to take a chance and bring Oprah to Chicago to pit against Phil Donahue in his own city.

Oprah was excited to accept the challenge and took advantage of the opportunity to move into a television market that reached a larger audience. She couldn't imagine that eighteen years later, she would still be reaching huge television audiences.

Oprah didn't want the station to try to change her, the way the Baltimore people had tried. She told Dennis Swanson, "I'm black and that's not going to change.

Oprah and Phil Donahue were no longer rivals when she presented him with an Emmy for Lifetime Achievement in 1996.

I'm overweight and that's probably not going to change either." Swanson responded, "You have a gift, a way of connecting with people. I don't expect you to change, just to use your gift."

Almost immediately, Oprah's gift captured the attention of the viewing audience. Within the month, *A.M. Chicago* had moved into first place in the Chicago area, beating Phil Donahue. Before Oprah became a national figure, *Newsweek* magazine wrote about her and her Chicago show. They described her as "nearly 200 pounds of Mississippi-bred black womanhood, brassy, earthy, street smart and soulful. . . ."

In the autumn of 1985, *A.M. Chicago* was renamed *The Oprah Winfrey Show*. The next year, the show started broadcasting nationally, with 138 stations signing up to air it.

Oprah skillfully moves among the people in her audience during a show.

Actress Whoopi Goldberg talks with director Steven Spielberg on the set of *The Color Purple*, Oprah's first film.

Oprah and Oscar

The Oprah Winfrey Show was just getting started when actor-musician-director-producer Quincy Jones happened to see it. Charmed with Oprah, he recommended her to Hollywood director Steven Spielberg for a role in the film *The Color Purple*, based on the novel by Alice Walker. Oprah played the role of Sofia, a woman who was battered and brutalized by the men in her life, but who managed to maintain her sense of humor and the value she placed on herself. For this first role in a film, Oprah was nominated for an Academy Award. She didn't win the Oscar, but she knew she had succeeded as an actress.

WHAT IS HER GIFT?

CHAPTER 5

"Use your gift," Dennis Swanson had told her. Her gift for getting people to tell their stories became an achievement of making it acceptable for people to talk about their feelings and problems. Through her discussions with her guests, Oprah demonstrates that everyone has problems and that having problems doesn't make a person "bad" or "strange." Viewers feel that Oprah is their friend, even though they don't personally know her. She seems to understand how guests and viewers feel. She advises her guests, "Just tell the truth. It'll save you, every time."

She took her own advice in the spring of 1986, when poet and author Maya Angelou appeared on Oprah's show. Angelou told about the time she had been raped at the age of seven. The event left her unable to speak for the next five years. Oprah then revealed to television audiences for the first time that she, too, had been raped

Good friends Maya Angelou (left) and Oprah Winfrey appeared together at a leadership conference in 2001.

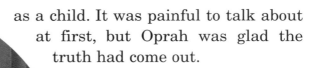

as a child. It was painful to talk about at first, but Oprah was glad the truth had come out.

THE ISSUE OF WEIGHT

Even after telling the truth, the sexual abuse of her young years still had serious lasting consequences for Oprah. It left her unable to accept that she was worthy of being loved, but it took her many years to realize that was what she felt deep down. Oprah knew only that she felt most comfortable when she was eating. Psychologists think that this feeling of not being lovable may be at the heart of many people's problems with weight.

The rapidly increasing audience of *The Oprah Winfrey Show* watched the host's weight go up and up. She began to speak about her problems with weight, sparking a dialogue between her and many other people with the same problem.

In 1988, fans watched as Oprah went on a diet in which she drank a special liquid instead of eating meals. She lost 67 pounds (30 kg). She stunned her audience by pulling a wagon containing sixty-seven pounds of fat onto the stage to demonstrate her accomplishment. She posed for magazine covers and marveled at her thinner body. Everyone else marveled and then also tried to diet that way, causing a giant increase in the liquid-diet business.

Like most people who took part in a liquid-diet program, Oprah very quickly regained the weight she had lost. She admits, however, that she didn't do any of the

Oprah had gained weight when this photo was taken in 1986. Weight has long been an issue for the TV star.

things she should have done to keep the weight off. (Scientists later announced that liquid diets could be dangerous.)

In the midst of her great success and increasing wealth, she still felt unhappy because of her weight. In 1992, she hired a personal trainer named Bob Greene to help her learn to exercise and lose weight. She spent an hour every morning with him, learning to jog, working on exercise machines, and lifting weights.

She was so successful that, in 1994, Oprah ran a marathon. The 26.2-mile (42-km) race took place in Washington, D.C. It was raining hard that day, and almost one-third of the runners dropped out, but not Oprah. Many people who watched the marathon that day were there just to cheer her on. "Life is a lot like a marathon," she says. "If you can finish a marathon, you can do anything you want."

Oprah showed off her new slender figure to the audience in 1988.

In the 1990s, Oprah learned to exercise and jog to keep her weight down. Here she is participating in a 1997 run/walk for women's cancer.

Taking Care of Business

For its first four years, Oprah's show was managed by a division of ABC Television, but by 1988, she took over the show's management. She put her friend, Jeffrey Jacobs, in charge of running her new management company, Harpo, Inc. "Harpo" is "Oprah" spelled backward.

Oprah built a production studio that takes up an entire city block in Chicago, just west of downtown. Oprah Winfrey tries to keep the number of employees fairly small (by entertainment standards) but feels free to move into any area of entertainment that interests her. Most of the employees of the company are women. Many of them are African American.

The Oprah Winfrey Show is created and filmed at Harpo studios in Chicago.

THE MAD-COW EPISODE

In spring of 1996, people in Europe became frightened of what came to be called mad-cow disease. They feared that they would contract a disease from beef that would make them crazy and eventually kill them. Millions of cattle throughout Europe were destroyed to keep the diseased beef from reaching the tables of consumers.

Kick Off Your Shoes

The Oprah Winfrey Show is a product of Oprah's personality. She leaves few decisions to other people. If she's not comfortable with the way things are going, she changes them. She says, "If I can't be myself and take my shoes off when my feet hurt, then I'm not going to do very well." And she has done just that—taken off her shoes in the middle of the show.

Oprah had a guest named Howard Lyman on her show. He claimed that American cattle were given feed containing ground-up diseased meat. (There has never been a case of mad-cow disease in the United States.) Winfrey inquired, "You said this disease could make AIDS look like the common cold?" When Lyman replied "Absolutely," Oprah blurted out, "It has just stopped me cold from eating another burger!"

Cattle prices dropped alarmingly during the next few days. Several cattlemen in Amarillo, Texas, sued Oprah, claiming that she had harmed the beef industry with her comment. She was facing charges of fraud, slander, defamation, and negligence, not to mention $100 million in damages. But more important to Oprah was that her **integrity** was being attacked.

Oprah's lawyers hired a firm called Courtroom Sciences, Inc. (SCI), to help prepare for the trial. A cofounder of SCI was a psychologist named Dr. Phillip McGraw. It was his job to work with Oprah to prepare her to answer anything that the lawyers for the cattle industry might ask.

Dr. Phillip McGraw with Oprah in Hollywood. After meeting the psychologist in Texas, she invited Dr. Phil to appear regularly on her show.

Oprah moved her entire show from Chicago to Amarillo, Texas, in late January 1998, so that she could continue doing her show during the time the trial took place. Late one night, Oprah began to panic about the whole problem and to feel sorry for herself. She knocked on Dr. McGraw's hotel door and moaned, "Why is this happening to me?" McGraw, who later wrote about the incident, said, "Oprah, look at me right now. You'd better wake up, girl, and wake up now. It is really happening. You'd better get over it and get in the game, or these good ole boys are going to hand you your ass on a platter."

Oprah's main defense in the trial was Freedom of Speech, which is guaranteed by the Bill of Rights. When one lawyer questioned her about the kinds of things discussed on her show, Oprah got angry and said, "I provide a forum for people to express their opinions. . . . This is the United States of America. We are allowed to do this in the United States of America."

Many people thought that because Amarillo is in the heart of the Texas cattle industry Oprah would lose the trial. But after two days of deliberations, the jury issued a verdict of "Not guilty!" An excited Oprah practically danced out of the courthouse.

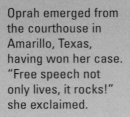

Oprah emerged from the courthouse in Amarillo, Texas, having won her case. "Free speech not only lives, it rocks!" she exclaimed.

For many people, the hour each weekday when Oprah airs is an important hour of the day. This secure audience has given Oprah a solid base from which to try many different things that interest her.

Oprah and Emmy

Oprah and her show have won many different Emmy Awards over the years. In 1998, Oprah was given an Emmy for Lifetime Achievement. It is very unusual for someone so young to win such an award. After receiving the Lifetime Achievement award, she withdrew her program from consideration for future Emmy Awards.

Oprah won many Emmy Awards for Daytime Television.

CHAPTER 6

THIS WILL CHANGE YOUR LIFE

"**M**y schedule is very hectic, but it's exactly the kind of life I've always wanted," Oprah says. "I've always said I wanted to be so busy that I wouldn't have time to breathe." She got what she wanted. Oprah has many facets to her busy life, including her efforts as a humanitarian, or a person who works toward the welfare of others. As soon as she gained financial wealth,

Political Action

Speaking from her own disturbed past as an abused child, Oprah Winfrey testified in 1991 before a committee of the U.S. Senate to support the creation of a national database of people who have been convicted of child abuse. The bill came to be called the "Oprah Bill." In1993, President Clinton signed it into law.

Oprah watches President Bill Clinton sign the 1993 Child Protection Act, known as the "Oprah Bill."

she established the Oprah Winfrey Foundation—a private charity that supports programs to inspire and educate women, children, and families.

In September 1997, Oprah announced the formation of Oprah's Angel Network. Her idea for the Network was to inspire people to use their lives to give to others. "I want you to open your hearts and see the world in a different way," said Oprah.

The Angel Network has always helped people in need, such as transporting sick children to hospitals.

She asked viewers to save their spare change and send it in. Oprah would match the money sent, and together they would fund scholarships for students who couldn't afford to go to college. In this first endeavor, Oprah's Angel Network collected more than $3.5 million. Millions more followed in later years.

The Angel Network has also worked to build homes and schools. More than two hundred homes for the organization called Habitat for Humanity have been built with Angel Network donations. Habitat for Humanity puts volunteers to work building houses for people who could otherwise not afford one.

Respecting Her Cause

In 2002, Oprah was chosen by the Academy of Television Arts and Sciences to receive the first-ever Bob Hope Humanitarian Award. The chairman said, "Oprah as an entertainer provokes thought, discussion, debate and empowers women, all in a graceful, direct, and honest style that we have all come to know and respect."

The first Bob Hope Humanitarian Award, given in 2002, went to Oprah Winfrey.

When twelve-year-old Craig Keilburger learned that millions of children all over the world must work from an early age and never go to school, he started an organization called Free the Children. He established a network of children to help children. They started by writing letters to public officials. Today, with the help of Oprah's Angel Network, they raise funds to help build schools. By the end of 2002, they had built thirty-four schools in ten countries.

Oprah's Angel Network also recognizes people who have made a difference in the lives of others through their charity work. The "Use Your Life Awards" donate money to many charitable organizations.

OPRAH AS GURU

"Guru" is a name given to a religious teacher and spiritual leader. People often use the word to describe any leader who helps people realize the best about themselves. Many people regard Oprah as their guru.

In 1997, Oprah realized that she could refresh herself and her show with a new approach. She looked back on her own life and saw the gradual changes she had

Within days after the September 11 attack on the World Trade Center in New York, First Lady Laura Bush appeared on *The Oprah Winfrey Show* to encourage parents to discuss the terrible event with their children.

made. All it took was her first decision to take responsibility for her own life. She realized that many people want to changes their lives, but they don't know how to get started. She decided to try and help those people with what she called "Change Your Life TV," special segments of *The Oprah Winfrey Show* with guests she believed could help guide her audience to leading better lives.

One of the first people she asked to be a part of "Change Your Life TV" was Dr. Phillip McGraw, who had helped her in Amarillo. Dr. Phil began appearing on Oprah's show every Tuesday. Oprah's audience on Tuesdays with Dr. Phil increased by almost one-fourth. People really wanted to hear what Dr. Phil had to say. In fact, his message encouraging listeners to take charge of their own lives was so popular that Oprah offered to produce Dr. Phil's own show for him.

Oprah produced and appeared in the 1993 film *There Are No Children Here.*

OPRAH AS ACTRESS, MOVIE PRODUCER, AND TEACHER

After her great success as Sofia in *The Color Purple* in 1985, Oprah was very careful in choosing the movies she would make. In fact, she was so careful that the only feature-length movies she has appeared in have been produced by her own company.

The film *Beloved* was a special project for Oprah. Based on a novel by Toni Morrison, *Beloved* tells the story of a former slave (played by Oprah) living in Ohio. This character is haunted by the ghost of a daughter that she killed so that the child wouldn't have to live in slavery. Oprah thought this film would be a great and influential success, but it was a failure with the public. She was so disappointed that she decided she would not act anymore. But she does produce films for others. In 1995, Oprah agreed to produce made-for-television movies for ABC-TV. She also plans to produce movies for Disney.

Oprah and Danny Glover in *Beloved*

Oprah in *The Women of Brewster Place*, which later became a TV show

Movie Appearances

Movies in which Oprah has appeared:

The Color Purple (1985)

Native Son (1986)

The Women of Brewster Place (1989)

There are No Children Here (1993)

Before Women Had Wings (1997)

Beloved (1998)

Oprah appears on the cover of each *O* magazine.

In 1999, Oprah spoke at the National Book Awards dinner.

In April 2000, Oprah introduced a monthly magazine called *O, The Oprah Magazine*, which is described as a personal-growth guide for the new century. About starting her own magazine, Oprah said: "What has been an advantage—even though some people might not consider it an advantage—is the fact that I had no magazine experience. Zip. Zilch. None. Zero. And so I came in with an open mind about what could and could not be done."

The magazine had the most successful start-up in history. Newstands everywhere sold out immediately, and they had to go back to press to produce hundreds of thousands more copies. Today, *O* has 2.2 million subscribers.

OPRAH AS READER

Books have always been important to Oprah. "Reading gave me hope," she said. "For me, it was the open door."

Because of her love of books, she often features writers and their recently published books on her program. At first, she invited writers to appear only occasionally. Then, in 1996, she began a regular monthly event on her show, Oprah's Book Club. She would invite an author to appear and have viewers join in a discussion about the book.

Suddenly, thousands were reading and buying the Oprah-selected books. It was later estimated that a selected book was guaranteed sales of half to three-quarters of a million copies, making them all bestsellers. The American Library Association (ALA) gave Oprah credit for "single-handedly expanding the size of the reading public." In fact, the ALA distributed many free copies of "Oprah's Books" to high school and public libraries.

Oprah received the 50th Anniversary Gold Medal from the National Book Foundation for her contribution to reading with Oprah's Book Club.

Three of writer Toni Morrison's novels have been selected for Oprah's Book Club. Sometimes Oprah has been accused of choosing Morrison's books because the two women are friends. Nonsense, responds Oprah, "Toni Morrison is the best writer, living or dead, and I love her work!"

In 2002, Oprah announced that she was stopping Oprah's Book Club. "It has become harder and harder," she said, "to find books on a monthly basis that I feel absolutely compelled to share." She said she was tired of reading contemporary books. Instead, she personally wants to return to reading classics.

The founders of the Oxygen cable network (from left): Marcy Carsey, Oprah, Geraldine Laybourne, and Caryn Mandabach. Carsey's production partner, Tom Werner, is also one of the founders.

Stedman Graham has been Oprah's important man for many years. Here they are at the 2001 Kennedy Center Honors in Washington, D.C.

Marcy Carsey and Tom Werner are known for creating television shows. In 1998, with Geraldine Laybourne, the founder of Nickelodeon, they formed Oxygen, a cable channel intended for women. Oprah Winfrey joined them as one of the owners. Oxygen began broadcasting in February 2000.

In the fall of 2002, Oprah began to broadcast on Oxygen a special half-hour called *Oprah After the Show*. After her regular hour-long program goes off the air, she continues to talk with her audience for another half-hour on Oxygen. *Oprah After the Show* is one reason many cable companies are picking up Oxygen.

OPRAH AS PRIVATE PERSON

Since 1986, Oprah has had one main man— Stedman Graham. Graham is an educator and businessman who grew up in New Jersey but attended Hardin Simmons University in Abilene, Texas, where he played basketball. He then went on to play in

Time to Relax

Oprah thought that she had to be working all the time in order to be worthy of love, but she finally began to learn that "all the money in the world doesn't mean a thing if you don't have time to enjoy it."

One way that she learned to relax was to buy a farm near Rolling Prairie, Indiana, a couple of hours drive from Chicago. She arranged her schedule so that she had to be in Chicago only a few days a week. The rest of the week she spends at her farm.

Gayle King is Oprah's best friend. No matter how busy the talk-show host is, she finds time to talk to her friend each day.

the European Basketball League. Coming home, he earned a graduate degree in education and worked in the education of convicts in prison. In the late 1980s, he started a marketing and public relations firm that deals primarily with sports figures.

OPRAH AT COLLEGE

In 2000, Oprah worked with Stedman Graham, teaching a course called the "Dynamics of Leadership" in the business school at Northwestern University.

Two years later, the University of Illinois began teaching the first course on Oprah herself. Dr. Juliet Walker, the professor offering "History 298: Oprah Winfrey, the Tycoon," says that studying Oprah "allows us to examine various aspects of American commerce and culture with greater clarity. She lives her life and does her show at the intersection of race, class, and gender—as well as entertainment and business. She is

Honoring Oprah

1987 First Emmy Award as outstanding talk show; eventually she and her show will receive a total of thirty-four Emmys

1988 International Radio and Television Society Broadcaster of the Year— youngest recipient ever

1993 Horatio Alger Award for overcoming poverty and other adversity

1994 Television Hall of Fame

1996 George Foster Peabody's Individual Achievement Award—the highest award in broadcasting

1997 *People* magazine names her as one of the fifty Most Beautiful People in the World

1998 *Time* magazine names her one of the 100 Most Influential People of the 20th Century

1998 Emmy for Lifetime Achievement by the Television Academy; voted the second most admired woman in the United States, behind Hillary Rodham Clinton

2001 *Newsweek* calls her "Woman of the Century"

2002 first Bob Hope Humanitarian Award

Oprah and her good friend Quincy Jones at the Oscars

Oprah the college professor spoke at Northwestern University's Kellogg Graduate School of Management in 2001 as chairperson of Harpo Entertainment Group.

Oprah Winfrey was following her vision of what she could accomplish when she launched *O, The Oprah Magazine*.

critical to understanding the position of black people in America today and the position of women in America today."

When Stedman Graham's daughter Wendy graduated from Wellesley College in 1997, Oprah gave the commencement address. One of the things she said reflects her whole life: "Create the highest, grandest vision possible for your life because you become what you believe."

Oprah has announced that she will stop *The Oprah Winfrey Show* in 2006. When Oprah was named to be one of *Time* magazine's 100 Most Influential People, Professor Deborah Tannen summed up the article about her this way: "She makes people care because she cares. That is Winfrey's genius, and will be her legacy. . . ."

TIMELINE

1954	Oprah Gail Winfrey is born on January 29 in Kosciusko, Mississippi
1960	Moves to Milwaukee, Wisconsin, to live with her mother
1968	Moves to Nashville, Tennessee, to live with her father
1970	Named Miss Fire Prevention; hired to read news on Nashville station WVOL Radio
1971	Graduates from East High School in Nashville; wins scholarship to Tennessee State University
1972	Named Miss Black Tennessee; becomes the first African-American anchor at WTVF-TV in Nashville
1973	Hired to anchor the evening news at Nashville's WTVF-TV
1976	Moves to Baltimore to coanchor the six o'clock news on WJZ-TV
1978	Cohosts WJZ-TV's local talk show, *People Are Talking*
1984	Moves to Chicago to cohost *A.M. Chicago* on WLS-TV
1985	*A.M. Chicago* is renamed *The Oprah Winfrey Show*; makes film debut as Sofia in *The Color Purple* ; nominated for an Academy Award as Best Supporting Actress
1986	*The Oprah Winfrey Show* is syndicated nationally
1988	Forms Harpo Productions, Inc. and takes ownership of her show
1991	Testifies before Congress to establish a national database of convicted child abusers; the National Child Protection Act is signed by President Clinton in 1993
1995	Named the only African American on *Forbes* magazine's list of the 400 richest Americans; runs a marathon (26.2 miles or 42 km) in Washington, D.C.
1996	Begins Oprah's Book Club
1997	Starts Oprah's Angel Network
1998	Helps create Oxygen Media, Inc.
2001	Publishes *O, The Oprah Magazine*
2002	Commits to keeping *The Oprah Winfrey Show* airing for several more years

GLOSSARY

abuse: physical, sexual, or mental mistreatment or cruelty

anchor: in a TV news program, the person who introduces reports and film clips by reporters

charitable: generous; meant to help other people

controversial: likely to cause an argument

forensics: public debate or speaking performance

ghetto: a section of a city where members of a single minority group tend to live (named after an island in ancient Venice where Jews were forced to live)

humanitarian: a person who works to improve the welfare of others

integration: the merging of two groups of people, such as African American and white students attending the same schools

integrity: an adherence to a code of ethics or values

premature: born too early in the pregnancy

production: in television, management of the creation of a program

raped: forced sexual activity on another person

social action: activities that are meant to help people out of difficult situations, such as poverty, abuse, and so on

tabloid: a newspaper that features stories (often not true) about violence, scandal, and personal lives of famous people

token: intending to show an absence of discrimination by having one member of a minority group included in a larger, mostly similar group

TO FIND OUT MORE

BOOKS

Brooks, Philip. *Oprah Winfrey: A Voice for the People.* Book Report Biography. Orchard Books, 1999.

Krohn, Katherine. *Oprah Winfrey.* First Avenue Editions, 2002.

Lowe, Janet. *Oprah Winfrey Speaks: Insights from the World's Most Influential Voice.* John Wiley & Sons, 2001.

Stone, Tanya Lee. *Oprah Winfrey: Success with an Open Heart.* Millbrook Press, 2001.

Ward, Kristin. *Learning About Assertiveness from the Life of Oprah Winfrey.* Character Building Books. Powerkids Press, 1999.

Wheeler, Jill C. *Oprah Winfrey.* Breaking Barriers series. Abdo & Daughters, 2002.

Wooten, Sarah McIntosh. *Oprah Winfrey: Talk Show Legend.* African-American Biographies. Enslow Publishers, 1999.

Woronoff, Kristen. *Oprah Winfrey: Media Superstar.* Library of Famous Women Juniors. Blackbirch Marketing, 2002.

INTERNET SITES

Oprah's official web site
http://www.oprah.com
Show and magazine information, as well as information about recent topics discussed on Oprah's TV show.

Oprah as a member of the American Academy of Achievement
http://www.achievement.org
Biographies of extraordinary individuals who have shaped our time.

Black History Month Biography
www.galegroup.com/free_resources/bhm/bio/winfrey_o.htm
Biography of this talk-show host, actress, and broadcasting executive.

About the Author

Jean F. Blashfield is the author of more than one hundred books, most of them for young people. During many years in publishing, she developed several encyclopedias; lived in London, England, where she edited books on nature; and started the book department at TSR, Inc., to create books for fans of the ever-popular *Dungeons & Dragons* game. She lives in Wisconsin where she delights in the fact that she becomes gripped by whatever subject she's writing about.